Proceed to Checkout

10 DEATH AFFIRMING PLAYS, SKETCHES AND MONOLOGUES

by Henry Meyerson

A SAMUEL FRENCH ACTING EDITION

SAMUEL FRENCH

FOUNDED 1830

NEW YORK HOLLYWOOD LONDON TORONTO

SAMUELFRENCH.COM

ISBN 978-0-573-69621-3   Printed in U.S.A.   #19045

IMPORTANT BILLING AND CREDIT REQUIREMENTS

All producers of *PROCEED TO CHECKOUT must* give credit to the Author of the Play in all programs distributed in connection with performances of the Play, and in all instances in which the title of the Play appears for the purposes of advertising, publicizing or otherwise exploiting the Play and/or a production. The name of the Author *must* appear on a separate line on which no other name appears, immediately following the title and *must* appear in size of type not less than fifty percent of the size of the title type.

In addition the following credit *must* be given in all programs and publicity information distributed in association with this piece:

AUTHOR'S NOTE

As with most collections of short works, the plays included in **PROCEED TO CHECK OUT** have had a checkered career. Some come from personal experience, some from re-worked short stories. All come from a mind obsessed with mortality. While some of these works were developed at New Jersey Dramatists and others at Time Square Playwrights, all were the result of mulling the message of Ecclesiastes who was such a downer he was rarely invited to parties.

Throughout these travails, I have relied on the support and wisdom of my wife, Ronnie, who is much funnier and has a better outlook on life than Ecclesiastes who, if you must know, can really bum you out big time if you take him seriously (maybe he was just upset with his name).

DOG YEARS

DOG YEARS premiered at the 2006 Samuel French Off Off Broadway Short Play Festival and was directed by Erin Woodward.

CAST

DOCTOR
PATIENT

PLACE

Psychiatrist's office

TIME

Present

SETTING

Two chairs, table between

(AT LIGHTS: **DOCTOR** *and* **PATIENT** *enter and sit.* **DOCTOR** *is holding a pad and pencil.)*

DOCTOR. So, how can I help you?

PATIENT. You can't.

DOCTOR. But you called for an appointment.

PATIENT. I did, but you won't be able to help me.

DOCTOR. How do you know that?

PATIENT. No one else has.

DOCTOR. So you've seen other therapists?

PATIENT. Big, small, male, female, white, black, fat, thin. All came out the same: *nada.*

DOCTOR. How many sessions do you usually have before terminating?

PATIENT. One.

DOCTOR. One?

PATIENT. Most times not even a whole one.

DOCTOR. But you keep trying. That's good.

PATIENT. If you say so. I keep trying, but I think it's futile.

DOCTOR. Let's begin by your telling me the problem.

PATIENT. Life is a series of disasters.

DOCTOR. Your life is a series of disasters?

PATIENT. No. Life in general. That's just the way life is: a series of disasters.

DOCTOR. When did you begin to feel this way?

PATIENT. When I was eight.

DOCTOR. So at eight years old you started to see life as a series of disasters.

PATIENT. No, at eight days.

DOCTOR. You remember when you were eight days old?

PATIENT. Like it was yesterday.

DOCTOR. What happened at eight days?

PATIENT. I lost a piece of my dick.

DOCTOR. Circumcision?

PATIENT. Mutilation.

DOCTOR. It happens to millions of little boys every day.

PATIENT. Exactly my point. Millions of defenseless little boys, barely able to hold their heads up, introduced to the world by being mutilated. Sounds like a disaster to me.

DOCTOR. But that was years ago. How old are you now?

PATIENT. Five.

DOCTOR. Five what?

PATIENT. Five years.

DOCTOR. You're a little large to be five years old.

PATIENT. About right, I would say.

DOCTOR. And precocious.

PATIENT. Thank you. Actually, I'll be five my next birthday.

DOCTOR. Even more impressive. Are you married?

PATIENT. Oh, sure. To Betty.

DOCTOR. Is she also five?

PATIENT. Thirty-five.

DOCTOR. So she married someone thirty years younger than herself.

PATIENT. When we got married I was actually older. But once I figured out what's what, I adopted dog years. She doesn't understand.

DOCTOR. You calculate your life in dog years?

PATIENT. You got it.

DOCTOR. Seven to one?

PATIENT. Approximately.

DOCTOR. What's the advantage of dog years?

PATIENT. You live longer. My aging one year for every seven of yours means I live seven times longer than you.

DOCTOR. But dogs usually die before they are fifteen.

PATIENT. Is that right?

DOCTOR. Last I heard.

PATIENT. You an expert on dogs?

DOCTOR. I used to own one.

PATIENT. How old when it died?

DOCTOR. After a full life, Jim died at thirteen.

PATIENT. Okay, what about tortoises? They live a long time.

DOCTOR. That's true, but I don't think you can pass your-self off as a tortoise.

PATIENT. You bought the dog idea.

DOCTOR. No, not really.

PATIENT. Another disaster in my life. See?

DOCTOR. Exactly what do you mean by disaster?

PATIENT. Alphabetical or just as they pop up in my mind?

DOCTOR. Free associate.

PATIENT. Tsunamis.

DOCTOR. We're in the middle of New Jersey. Little chance of a tsunami here.

PATIENT. How about cancer?

DOCTOR. Okay, I'll give you that.

PATIENT. Heart disease, liver disease.

DOCTOR. Okay. I'll give you those.

(During the following monologue **DOCTOR** *becomes increasing depressed and haunted looking, possibly sinking into his chair, covering his head as if to protect himself.)*

PATIENT. Hurricanes, typhoons, cyclones, nor'easters, bankruptcy, automobile accident, plane crash, being hit by a truck or bus or car or motorcycle, getting a lawyer's letter, walking down the street and being hit in the head by a safe someone threw out of a window, terrorist attack, being attacked by a rabid dog, being attacked by several rabid dogs, bats flying into your hair, rats gnawing at your toes, ingrown toe nail, razor cuts, insurance agents, lice, dirty bombs, clean bombs, any kind of bombs, salmonella, botchellism, AIDS, all manner of broken bones, all manner of illnesses and diseases not yet mentioned, not knowing which of my cells might turn traitor and mutate into some hideous malformation causing agonizing pain and death, the heartache and the thousand natural shocks that flesh is heir to...

(**DOCTOR** *cracks his pencil in half. He is quivering in fear.*)

DOCTOR. STOP. Enough. I get it.

PATIENT. I've made my point, then.

DOCTOR. YES, yes, clearly you've made your point.

PATIENT. How long have you been in practice, Doc?

DOCTOR. Five years.

PATIENT. How old are you now?

DOCTOR. I'll be six my next birthday.

PATIENT. I think we've made a breakthrough here, Doc. Put me down for next week.

The End

COMRADES

COMRADES was originally published as "What are Comrades For?", a short story by the playwright, in both *The New Jersey Review* and *Rosebud Magazine*.

CAST

FYODOR
IVAN

PLACE

Hospital room, Russia

TIME

1857 or 1858. Summer. Maybe July. Anyway, it's hot.

SETTING

A hospital room with one chair and a bed containing **FYODOR**. **FYODOR** is cover by a blanket to his neck. His head is swathed in bandages, his mouth covered. Only eye holes break through to the human inside the bandages.

(AT LIGHTS: **IVAN** *enters and sits on a chair.)*

IVAN. Fyodor, it is me, your best friend, Ivan.

FYODOR. Grmplxy.

IVAN. No problem. I'm only too glad to come and keep you company in this trying time. But I must tell you, Fyodor, you have made a big mistake. It is not right what you have done. It is against nature.

FYODOR. Mmph. Ngr. Hphm

IVAN. Yes, yes, easy for you to say, but it is us, your dear friends, who now suffer because of what you have done. Placing yourself in the path of the Muscovy Express may have been part of your grand scheme to suffer, but you never stopped to consider the effects. You wish to suffer, well, then, you will suffer. I, too, am suffering. It is hot and smells bad in here. My back and my feet ache. I am hungry and thirsty. But the worst, Fyodor is that you refuse to discuss this lunacy of yours.

FYODOR. Mgrsh ngphsh bglch fmfm.

IVAN. That is not the point, and I am tired of having to listen to your endless prattle about your guilt. We all have guilt. I, myself, am just now feeling guilt that I am having lustful thoughts about your wife now that you are immobilized. But you don't see me step in front of a train, do you, you stupid potato eater? Do you realize the position you have put me in. On the one hand you are my dearest friend and I want you to get well, but on the other hand I also know if you died I could be on top of Sophia in a matter of moments. This is a terrible predicament you've placed me in.

FYODOR. Mgrsh ngphsh bglch fmfm.

IVAN. Yes, yes, please, you have already said that. It is difficult enough to sit here. Please don't repeat yourself. But, in all candor, of course, you are right. I was behaving like a peasant. Boorish, I think you said. That you are my oldest friend. That I should not behave lustfully with your wife. But Fyodor, my old friend, I have it on good authority you had behaved in a like manner with Dimitri. Although that was with Dimitri's daughter, come to think of it. So if I am a peasant, then there is an old peasant saying, "What's good for the Fyodor is good for the Ivan."

FYODOR. Grph, ngh vlat wbgrh.

IVAN. Well, but don't you think that is up to her? After all, Sophia is a grown woman. And it's not like you have been all that attentive as a husband. We are all well aware, Fyodor, of how you spend your time. Teaching those young boys. What exactly do you teach them, eh, my good friend? Spiritual matters, no doubt. I can just picture you now saying to your students, "Yes, that's the spirit." Spirit, indeed. Spurt is more like it. No, no don't move. You must remain calm, my friend. I am here to help you. What is it that you need?

FYODOR. Ngorph hcgqua frmono.

IVAN. Ah, my friend, I am afraid there is little I can do on that score. But, I must get to the point. I am here as the bearer of bad news. Since your most recent run in with the train you have gone through all of your funds. The short of it is, you are broke. You can image what this is all costing. Sophia tried to pawn her brooch, but the old pawnbroker – do you recall her – was murdered by some crazed student and so is no longer in business. Poor Sophia has been forced to return to her old line of work. Yes, imagine, back to the way you met her. She even has her old spot under the lamp post. But after all, what was she to do? Also, she has been forced to put Maria, Ivan, Natasha and Maximilian into the foster home. There are just too many children, Fyodor, you old dog. As your old friend, I helped Sophia compose a letter that we sent off to your parents asking for help. But Siberia is so far away, and then of course there is the difficulty in getting the letter into the camp. And then once it finally arrives, in reality there is so little they can do. Are you listening, Fyodor? It is difficult to tell, what with your face covered over like that. I keep imagining that you are nodding off.

FYODOR. Frascis nemblech niblich.

IVAN. Truly you are a remarkable person. After all you have been through, to still want to help your family through this ordeal is quite commendable. No, no, it is obvious you are in no shape to offer any assistance. But, listen, Fyodor, the real tragedy here for me is all of this could have been avoided if you had only stuck to your writing instead of filling your head with theories, theories, and more useless theories. It is all of this useless thinking that has gotten you into this mess: every bone broken, face smashed, penniless, wife on the street, children abandoned, parents arrested. Ah well, fortunately you still have me, eh. Well, I must be off. I will be seeing your wife. Any message?

FYODOR. Grmph ngmt.

IVAN. Right. Well, 'til tomorrow. *(to O.S)* Oh nurse, hello, I was just about to leave. Tell me, it is alright for me to sit and keep Fyodor company this long, isn't it? *(beat)* This is not Fyodor? Ah, this is Mr. Nezikov. But Fyodor?... died yesterday. *(beat)* Ah, so at least no more suffering for poor Fyodor, eh? Well, goodbye Mr. Nezikov. I'll see you tomorrow.

NEZIKOV. Frzbh mgrpg noowgh.

IVAN. No, no. Think nothing of it. My pleasure.

The End

THE SUITCASE

THE SUITCASE premiered at New Jersey Dramatists 2003 One Act Festival and was directed by Mikaela Kafka. It was then performed at Teachers Theatre's 2004 One Act Festival where it was directed by Jewel Seehaus-Fisher and at Manhattan Playwrights, Inc.'s 2004 Short Cuts, directed by Jenn Bornstein.

CAST

JACK - Around 70
BARBARA - Jack's daughter
STEVE - Barbara's husband
SUZY - Funeral home salesperson

PLACE

Florida funeral home

TIME

Now

SETTING

Table, four chairs

(AT LIGHTS: **JACK**, **BARBARA** *and* **STEVE** *sit at the table.
Throughout,* **BARBARA** *occasionally sniffles and dabs
her eyes as they tear.)*

JACK. What's taking so long?

BARBARA. We're waiting.

JACK. For who?

STEVE. Ted.

JACK. Oh, right. You told me.

STEVE. Ten times we told you.

BARBARA. Calm down.

STEVE. This is calm.

BARBARA. This is not easy on him.

STEVE. Who is this easy on, Barbara? Tell me.

JACK. I'll pack when we get back to the house.

BARBARA. You have plenty of time to pack.

JACK. I'll have to find the suitcase.

STEVE. You're not going until tomorrow. Enough all ready
with the packing.

JACK. I'll pack enough for a couple of days. *(beat)* What's
taking them so long. *(beat)* What's his name, again?

STEVE. I can't take it. I'm going for a walk.

*(**STEVE** stands.)*

BARBARA. *(to* **STEVE***)* Oh, no, you don't. You can't leave
me with this. Sit down. *(to* **JACK***)* Ted. And he's only a
couple of minutes late.

*(**STEVE** sits.)*

JACK. Seems longer.

STEVE. *(irritated)* That's because we got here an hour early.

BARBARA. *(to* **STEVE***)* Can you please stop this? Leave him…

JACK. I didn't want to be late.

STEVE. At this point a half-hour one way or the other isn't going to make much of a difference.

JACK. She was a wonderful woman, Steve.

STEVE. I understand.

JACK. She loved you like her own son. You, too, Barbara.

STEVE. We know.

BARBARA. Why don't you sit down, Dad.

(**JACK** *sits.* **SUZY** *enter.*)

SUZY. I apologize for keeping you waiting. Sorry for the mix up.

BARBARA. What mix up and who are you?

SUZY. Suzy.

BARBARA. You're not Ted.

SUZY. I'm Suzy. I'm here to help you make arrangements for the burial of your loved one.

STEVE. We were supposed to see Ted.

SUZY. I'll be able to help you with the arrangements.

BARBARA. I spoke to Ted on the phone last night and he said he would be here this morning to help us. I don't want to have to go through all this again with someone new.

SUZY. Ted had an emergency.

STEVE. Emergency? What could be more of an emergency than this?

SUZY. I understand. But it was something that just came up.

JACK. *(to* **BARBARA***)* Is that...? Who were we supposed to meet again?

BARBARA. Ted.

JACK. Oh, right. *(to* **SUZY***)* Ted, I'm Jack. We're here to arrange for my wife's funeral. She died yesterday...

SUZY. That's why I'm here. To help facilitate the funeral. And I'm not Ted.

JACK. Then who are you?

SUZY. Suzy.

JACK. *(to* BARBARA*)* I thought we were waiting for Ted.

STEVE. I'm feeling a little tense right now. I need some air. Can we open a window?

SUZY. Maybe we should just focus on the arrangements.

JACK. Where's Ted?

SUZY. There was an emergency walk-in and he had to handle it.

STEVE. What kind of emergency would walk into a place like this? Someone dies, you call, you come in the next day. Isn't that how it works?

SUZY. It was an emergency.

STEVE. *(slowly, calmly)* Suzy, so we're all on the same page, let me explain. I'm Steve. This is my wife, Barbara. This is her father, Jack.

SUZY. Pleasure.

STEVE. Pleasure? How could this be a pleasure?

SUZY. I didn't quite mean...

STEVE. *(slowly, but with increasing anger so that at the end, he is yelling)* See, we're here because Edith, Barbara's mother, Jack's wife, died yesterday and we thought, silly us, that this funeral home might be able to help us out. Ted, the man with the emergency more important than ours, was supposed to meet us here. We even had an appointment, but now that I understand how this works, maybe we should have just "walked in," perhaps carrying Edith in our arms, then we would have had the courtesy of getting THE SERVICE WE EXPECTED.

SUZY. I understand your concern, and believe me, I am very sympathetic to your loss of Mrs., Mrs. *(She searches through her papers.)*, er...

JACK. I think one suitcase would be enough. The medium sized one.

SUZY. *(pronounces it Weinsteen)* Mrs. Weinstein.

BARBARA. *(with anger, correcting her pronunciation)* Weinstein. You don't even know her name. I think that's the least...

SUZY. I'm sorry. Weinstein.

STEVE. Are you as qualified as Ted to do this?

SUZY. Oh, yes. Although, I must admit, Ted is stronger at grief counselling, whereas, my strength is in book-keeping.

STEVE. We're not doing an audit, Suzy. We are doing grief. No offence, but get Ted.

SUZY. *(pause)* To be perfectly frank, there was no emergency walk-in. Ted had a hell of a night last night and he couldn't make it into work today.

BARBARA. So, you're it?

STEVE. Because Ted got loaded?

SUZY. And ran his car into a ditch.

BARBARA. Unbelievable.

SUZY. Not really if you knew Ted.

BARBARA. I meant...never mind.

STEVE. *(to SUZY)* Quick, what's the deceased name?

SUZY. *(pronounces it correctly)* Mrs. Weinstein.

STEVE. Now we're cookin'. Right, Barb? Clear sailing.

JACK. She was a wonderful woman.

SUZY. *(mechanically insincere)* I'm sure she was, Mr. Weinstein. This is a very great loss. And you have our sincerest sympathies.

JACK. *(crying)* A wonderful woman.

SUZY. *(mechanically insincere)* I'm sure she was, Mr. Weinstein. This is a very great loss. And you have our sincerest sympathies.

JACK. Thank you.

STEVE. I know I'm touched. How about you, Barb?

BARBARA. Let's keep this moving, Steve.

SUZY. As I understand it, you're planning to send your wife to New York.

JACK. We have plots on Long Island. They're all paid up. Caskets, plots, even the travel costs. We didn't want to cost my kids anything. My wife, she made sure there wouldn't be any foul-up.

SUZY. I'm sure Mrs. Weinstein…*(mispronounced)*

BARBARA. *(correcting her pronunciation)* Weinstein.

SUZY. …Weinstein was very thoughtful and efficient. Which cemetery?

JACK. It was on Long Island someplace. I don't remember…

SUZY. Pinelawn Cemetery

JACK. Right. Pinelawn. I'm sorry. I'm just not thinking too good right now.

STEVE. *(to SUZY)* How did you…?

SUZY. Lot of folks here in Fort Lauderdale have plots in Long Island and I handle the money, so…

STEVE. Of course. What did you do before funerals, Suzy?

SUZY. Used cars. Before that, real estate.

STEVE. I'll bet you know your way around sales, right?

JACK. She wanted to go back north. She was a wonderful woman,

SUZY. *(mechanically insincere)* I'm sure she was, Mr. Weinstein. This is a very great loss. And you have our sincerest sympathies.

JACK. Thank you.

SUZY. *(to JACK)* This is a very trying time for you. *(beat)* So…I'm not sure I should bring this up, but…

STEVE. Then don't.

SUZY. *(to JACK)* I just think you should consider your options.

STEVE. What options? There are no options. My mother-in-law died, she needs to be buried. Where's the option in that? Resurrection?

SUZY. I know the original plan was sending the body to Pinelawn, but…

STEVE. Original plan? There is no plan B, Suzy, so don't even go there.

SUZY. *(to JACK)* I wouldn't want you to make a mistake and be sorry later.

STEVE. You want to help out here, Barbara? I see a train wreck coming.

BARBARA. I think we should hear her out, Steve. We don't want Dad to feel he made a mistake.

STEVE. About what? This was all neatly arranged. Paaaid fooor and arranged. Get it now?

SUZY. You know, Mr. Weinstein, I have some material in my office you might find interesting. Want to take a look?

JACK. Sure, why not?

STEVE. Dad, wait…

(SUZY and JACK exit.)

You see what's happening here? He's vulnerable and she's a shark.

BARBARA. Is this about you or Dad?

STEVE. What's that supposed to…?

BARBARA. You're taking this as if she was personally attacking you.

STEVE. Us. She's personally attacking *us* and is about to gobble him up. She wants to sell him…I don't even know what she wants to sell him, but I'm sure it's a beaut.

BARBARA. Whatever it is, we can afford it.

STEVE. It isn't about the money.

BARBARA. Then what?

STEVE. Because he's a nice old guy who just lost his wife, and you're a nice daughter who just lost her mother and Suzy is a used car hustler moving in to close a deal.

BARBARA. Nice old guy? That's it?

STEVE. Okay, I love him like he was my own father and I don't want him taken advantage of. Okay?

BARBARA. Okay. That's better, but I think we should let him decide what…

(SUZY and JACK enter.)

JACK. I've been thinking.

STEVE. That right?

JACK. I know Mom wanted to be buried on Long Island so she could be with her parents, but maybe…I don't know…

BARBARA. What, Dad?

JACK. Well, Suzy pointed out if Mom stayed here in Florida I could visit her, but if she went up north…

STEVE. You and Suzy had quite a discussion.

JACK. But, as Suzy pointed out, if Mom stayed here I'd have to get two plots down here…

STEVE. Why two?

JACK. One for Mom and one for me for later, and a new coffin. That's a lot of money, Barbara.

STEVE. Yes, it is, isn't it.

BARBARA. Don't worry about the money. We'll pay for it, Dad. Right, Steve?

JACK. Yeah, that might be better. Then I won't have to pack a suitcase.

BARBARA. Steve?

STEVE. *(gives up)* Yeah, I guess that might be better.

(All turn to **SUZY** *who picks up the calculator.)*

SUZY. Will you be putting this on your charge?

The End

THE STRUGGLE

CAST

ACTOR

SETTING

Bare stage

(AT LIGHTS: **ACTOR** *enters.)*

ACTOR. It's been just about a year since I visited my mother in an intensive care unit. Even if you're not a patient an ICU can be a strange and scary place. At first it was hard to tell where my mother began and the bed ended. By then, two days into her struggle, it was as if the white of the pillow-case and sheet had crept under her skin. She lay in this bed with a pipe crammed into her mouth taped to her jaw. Her eyes were slammed shut. But it was the noise: Pssssh, thummmm, pssssh, thummmm, pssssh, thummmm that really caught my attention. With each pssssh, the air driven into her lungs through the tube wedged into her mouth caused her chest to heave out like some startled balloon. With each thummmm, the air in her lungs was sucked out, back down through the tube, collapsing her chest, deflating her, rolling her flat under the sheet like a cartoon character run over by a steam roller. She was "Pneumatic Woman," and she didn't look much like the mother I had known. *(beat)* The room was a large, windowless, circular masterpiece of technology. It was lit with what seemed to be a year's voltage from the Hoover Dam. Around the wall, feet toward the center of the room, the patients lay like spokes on a wheel, each surrounded by blindingly white curtains to create cubicles, each crammed full of electrical gadgetry: woofers, tweeters, polished aluminum, diodes, cathodes, and Pentium chips, beeping, gurgling, woofing and tweeting, all overseen by efficient well-trained nurse/technician/blast-off facilitators whose job it was to make sure all systems, vascular, renal, neurological, digestive, and coronary, were "go." *(beat)* The one tending my mother had curly blond hair, large gray eyes, a radiant, effervescent smile; the perky, bouncy stuff of cheerleaders. She was a dish and she was my dilemma. Mother with her pssssshing and thummmming, Dish with her smiling and prancing, certainly one was more compelling and needed my attention. Ah, but which one? *(beat)* Margaret, the woman in the bed, had been my mother for nearly forty [*age can be changed to accommodate actor*] years. What I'll remember was her humor, her savage rages, her self-pity, and her complete devotion to her family. What I'll remember will make me crazy trying to sort it all out. But she had some humor. If I said her life was a paradox, she'd say, "If you're lucky, it's a three a dox." Then I'd say, "Sometimes it's a three of spades." Then she'd say... I don't remember any more what she would say. *(beat)* I asked nurse Dish, "How's she doing?" "That your mother?" she asked back. Nurse Dish had a voice that floated on a cloud, that wafted to me from ethereal regions inhabited by Eleusinian creatures mortals only surmised existed. That it passed through her nose and resonated in her sinuses giving her the sound of a Scottish bagpipe only added to its charm. "Yup, that's my mother. Has there been any change?" said I. (And will you have dinner and passionate sex with me?) "No, pretty much the same," nurse Dish whined, perking up her tiny nose. "She's such a dear lady. I sure hope she gets better." I thanked her, but she was wrong about that. That woman lying with the tube down her throat, pssssshing and thummmming, was not "pretty much the same." She was worse with each passing moment because the longer she stayed in a coma the worse her prognosis and nurse Dish didn't really give a shit if my mother got better or not because Dish's life wasn't going to change whatever happened to my mother. Now, about dinner. *(beat)* Here's some irony. "Florida," Mom would say. "My future is in Florida." Well, she was certainly right about that, because to Florida she went, lived a few years, then returned to New York her future behind her, a crippled, despondent old woman, who was about to die. So her being in that place at that

time made perfect sense. What didn't make sense was
the nurse. What the hell was this Dish doing here, with
her curls, her dimples, her goddamn gray eyes distract-
ing my mourning? She was starting to piss me off. I
asked her if it was okay for me to stay here awhile. "Oh
sure," she said. "Stay as long as you like. You ain't both-
erin' nobody." She smiled: whimsical, ironic, satirical,
who could tell, who could fathom her depths, her
dimples, her gray eyes, her white uniform that hugged
her ass like a tourniquet? Psssh, thummm. Was that
a change? *(beat)* My mother was old all her life. Born
into it, you might say. Photographs of her even when
she was young show a woman who had the weight of
the world on her shoulders, head, back, thighs, every-
where. Atlas had it easy. *(beat)* Not that Dish's life was a
bowl of cherries. Plug this into that, monitor this print
out, titrate that drip, drip this titrate. Busy, busy, busy.
In fact, I could have stayed there all day and watched
her as she bent, stretched, wriggled and fussed. It was
quite a show. Pssh, thumm. "She's psshing and thum-
ming a little less, don't you think, nurse? I'm sorry I
didn't get your name," I said. "Debby," she said and
then Dish Debby discovered one of the electrical leads
to the bellows that pushed the air into my mother's
lungs had frayed. She called an electrician. Bit of irony
here. My mother thought of herself as handy around
wiring. Lamps, outlets, cars, if it had electric she was
your fixer. If she wasn't at that very moment otherwise
currently (no pun intended) occupied, she'd be Margaret on the spot trying to straighten out the problem.
Now, of course, the problem was happening to her.
Psh, thum. Things were getting serious. "Oh, nurse."
"I think something might be wrong with the coolant,"
she said, "I called a plumber." First an electrician,
now a plumber. Dish was like a contractor hired to
over-see a construction site. She was very helpful and
considerate especially when she bent over my mother
to straighten the tubing in her throat. "Don't worry,
she doesn't feel that," she said. Wasn't that amazing?

Dish was also able to experience other people's pain.
I wondered if she could read minds. Could she have
known that when my mother died I would be relieved,
I would be free of having to fail, of having to subject
myself to life's humiliations, that I would be free of
her oppression, of her having wormed herself into
my gut so that by now we are one under the skin, that
when she died I would be free to wail and bemoan
the loss of the woman who gave up her egg to bring
me into this world? Could nurse Dish have known I'd
make sure the dinner was over quickly so I could get
her back to my apartment? Psh...BEEEEEEEEEEEEP
came over the speaker as running footsteps sounded
behind me. Dish Debby drew the curtains around my
mother while peering out at me as if she was about to
engage in something illicit with the old lady. Someone
gently walked me to the door. Dinner with nurse Dish
was definitely off.

The End

LUCKY MAN

LUCKY MAN premiered *(titled: BEWARE THE LIVING WILL)* at the 2007 Bloomington Playwrights' Sex and Death One Act Festival.

CAST

MR. SMITH
MS. SMITH
DOCTOR

PLACE

Doctor's office

TIME

Present

SETTING

Desk and chair, another two chairs facing desk

(AT LIGHTS: **SMITH** *and* **MRS. SMITH** *are seated in the two chairs facing the desk.)*

SMITH. What do you think he'll say?

MRS. SMITH. He will say that it's nothing to worry about. Stop carrying on so.

SMITH. Easy for you to say. You're not the one who has had to put up with all of this.

MRS. SMITH. You always make too much out of things. Mountains out of molehills.

SMITH. Maybe you're right.

MRS. SMITH. Of course. You shouldn't be so pessimistic. *(sings)* "Always look on the bright side of life." I always loved that song.

SMITH. I'll try, but...

*(***DOCTOR*** enters. He is wearing a white doctor's coat.)*

DOCTOR. Well, Mr. Smith, the test results have come back, but I'm afraid they are still inconclusive.

SMITH. *(to* **MRS. SMITH***)* See, I told you.

MRS. SMITH. That doesn't mean there is anything wrong. All that means is they just don't know what's wrong.

DOCTOR. Exactly. Your wife has put her finger right on the crux of the problem. We just don't know. Very good, Mrs. Smith.

MRS. SMITH. Thank you, Doctor.

SMITH. Then what is the next step? I can't continue to live like this.

MRS. SMITH. Don't mind him, Doctor. He tends to over-dramatize.

DOCTOR. No, Mrs. Smith, I think Mr. Smith's question is perfectly reasonable.

SMITH. *(to* **MRS. SMITH***)* See.

DOCTOR. And I have a perfectly reasonable answer to your perfectly reasonable question regarding the next step. I have discussed your puzzling case with all of the other doctors at the hospital and they all agree we cannot allow this situation to continue.

SMITH. Great. So what do we do?

DOCTOR. We do an autopsy.

(There is silence for a while as the SMITHS absorb the news.)

SMITH. Autopsy?

DOCTOR. The sooner the better. That way we'll know exactly what we're dealing with.

MRS. SMITH. See, I told you there was nothing to worry about, that the doctors have everything in hand.

SMITH. I think there's been a mistake.

MRS. SMITH. So when does this take place?

DOCTOR. I've cleared my calendar for the rest of the day to take care of this. How about it, Mr. Smith?

MRS. SMITH. Hear that, dear? The doctor has cleared his calendar just to take care of you.

SMITH. Autopsy?

DOCTOR. Don't look so worried, Mr. Smith. I've performed thousands of these. Nothing to it.

MRS. SMITH. I keep telling him that he makes too big a deal out of nothing.

DOCTOR. Your wife is right, Mr. Smith. You must lighten up.

SMITH. Autopsy?

MRS. SMITH. See, Doctor. This is what I have to deal with day after day. This negativism.

DOCTOR. Not an uncommon reaction in these situations, Mrs. Smith.

MRS. SMITH. *(to DOCTOR)* Oh, I'm just sick of it. Here you go ahead and clear your calendar, take all this time out of your valuable schedule, and what does he do? He just sits there like some frog on a log repeating the same word over and over. *(to* **SMITH***)* Ribbit, ribbit.

SMITH. Autopsy?

MRS. SMITH. See?

DOCTOR. What is the problem, Mr. Smith?

SMITH. I thought autopsies are done after a person dies.

DOCTOR. Well, that's true in most cases.

SMITH. But I'm not dead.

DOCTOR. That is also true.

SMITH. Then…

DOCTOR. Because your case is so unusual, we here at the hospital have decided to make an exception.

SMITH. I refuse to…

DOCTOR. Have you, or have you not, written a living will?

SMITH. Well, yes, but…

MRS. SMITH. It was my idea. What with all the political hoo ha and courts and politicians getting into the act, I felt this was a family matter. He didn't want to, but I made him.

DOCTOR. Good for you, Mrs. Smith.

MRS. SMITH. Thank you, Doctor.

DOCTOR. *(to* **SMITH***)* And this living will, does it, or does it not, allow your wife, the beautiful and clever Mrs. Smith, to make decisions regarding your health in critical situations?

SMITH. Well, yes, but…

DOCTOR. Is this, or is this not, a critical situation?

SMITH. Well, maybe, but…

DOCTOR. Mrs. Smith?

MRS. SMITH. Seems critical to me. He's been bellyaching about his condition for months. I, for one, am fed up with it.

DOCTOR. Therefore, Mrs. Smith…?

MRS. SMITH. Go for it, I say.

DOCTOR. Good girl!

(**DOCTOR** *leaps on* **SMITH** *and drags him, kicking and struggling, O.S.* **MRS. SMITH** *sits placidly waiting, whistling the "Bright side" tune, as we hear* **SMITH** *screaming O.S.* **DOCTOR** *enters, his white coat bloody, holding a lump of meat.*)

DOCTOR. Your husband was absolutely correct, Mrs. Smith. He was a very sick man. Look at this *(hold out meat for her inspection)* It was buried so deeply in his abdomen we never would have found it without an autopsy.

MRS. SMITH. Lucky he signed that living will.

DOCTOR. He's lucky he had a wife who cared enough to make him.

MRS. SMITH. Will he be all right?

DOCTOR. He would have, had he survived the autopsy *(throws meat on table).*

MRS. SMITH. Dead, then?

DOCTOR. 'fraid so.

MRS. SMITH. Well, these things happen. At least I got him to sign up for a whopper of a life insurance policy.

DOCTOR. First the living will, and now the life insurance? You are the clever little woman, aren't you?

MRS. SMITH. Mother always told me to tend to my knitting.

DOCTOR. I'm heading uptown. Care to join me for coffee?

MRS. SMITH. Might as well. Don't have much else planned.

(Both exit. Lights out.)

The End

REHEARSAL

CAST

ARCHIE
BETTY

TIME

Now

PLACE

Anywhere

SETTING

Bare stage. Two chairs, table. Chessboard on table.

(AT LIGHTS: **BETTY** *and* **ARCHIE** *are seated at a table playing chess. There is silence as they contemplate the board.* **ARCHIE** *makes a move.)*

BETTY. Interesting move, Archie.

ARCHIE. Thank you, Betty.

BETTY. You realize this places you in a very precarious position.

ARCHIE. I live for danger.

BETTY. I meant on the board, not in life.

ARCHIE. There is no metaphor for life, Betty. Life is life. I don't mistake chess for life. Sixty-four squares, thirty-two pieces, two sides. Chess is immutable. Life, on the other hand…

BETTY. Yes?

ARCHIE. …is much different. Make your move.

*(***BETTY*** *moves a piece.)*

BETTY. Well, in certain respects life is immutable.

ARCHIE. Such as?

BETTY. Babies keep being born. And, of course, eventually we die.

ARCHIE. Looked at that way, I would have to agree. So, immutable it is. Shall we continue?

(They stare at the board.)

Do you find this game sufficient?

BETTY. No, not really.

ARCHIE. Neither do I. Not much meaning.

BETTY. You want meaning? I thought we had worked this through.

ARCHIE. I was hoping.

BETTY. *(incredulous)* Hoping? Hoping?

ARCHIE. Actually, I was hoping to hope.

BETTY. *(soothing)* Archie, Archie.

ARCHIE. *(hopefully)* Suppose we play with our eyes closed.

BETTY. You sound hopeful.

ARCHIE. No, not hopeful. I was aiming for eager.

BETTY. I just don't want you to be hurt again.

ARCHIE. And I appreciate that, Betty.

BETTY. Archie, whenever you've reached out into the unknown for some ray of hope deep down you harbored a longing for something that can never be. And you will, as in the past, feel the sting of defeat, the pain of rejection, the anguish of unfulfillment. In other words, Archie, forgetaboutit.

ARCHIE. Thank you, Betty. It is comforting to know you care.

BETTY. *(as in: blah, blah, blah)* ...right, right, right, blind chess, huh?

ARCHIE. Exactly.

BETTY. I thought you didn't believe in metaphors of life.

ARCHIE. I see what you mean.

BETTY. Leaves us in a quandary, then.

ARCHIE. Isn't a quandary a place where people dig rock.

BETTY. I think people dig rock in concert halls. It used to be rock clubs, but the acts got too expensive.

ARCHIE. Have we switched from playing chess to playing with words.

BETTY. It was too good a segue to pass up.

ARCHIE. Can I try one?

BETTY. Of course, there are no rules.

    (**ARCHIE** *thinks long and hard.*)

ARCHIE. Can't think of any.

BETTY. It'll come. Can't force these things, Arch. Sometimes words and ideas come up when you least expect them. I understand the same thing happens to a lot of great writers. Can we get back to the chess?

    (*They contemplate the chess board.*)

ARCHIE. Nope, this chess thing still isn't working.

BETTY. Yeah. Not enough zip.

ARCHIE. Zip would be good, but I don't think chess is zippy.

BETTY. Maybe we need a whole new approach.

ARCHIE. You're right. Okay, let's start over.

BETTY. From the beginning?

ARCHIE. Exactly.

BETTY. Me or you?

ARCHIE. I think it was you last time, wasn't it?

BETTY. Right you are. Ready?

ARCHIE. Shoot.

> (**BETTY** *pulls a gun and shoots* **ARCHIE** *who falls back in his seat.* **BETTY** *puts away the gun and waits. She becomes impatient, tapping her fingers, looking at her watch, squirming, etc.* **ARCHIE** *revives.*)

BETTY. Ah, there you are.

ARCHIE. Always have been, as far as I can tell. Were you worried?

BETTY. You did take a rather long time. I think you overdid this one.

ARCHIE. Trying to get the feel of it, you know. You want to get it right.

BETTY. Well, I think this is one performance that's hard to get wrong. Besides, it's not as if you're going to have a long run with this. It's a one shot deal. Up and out.

ARCHIE. I've always felt it better to rehearse and get it right. Considering the importance, all the more reason we have to nail its premiere.

BETTY. Seems to me as if you nailed it.

ARCHIE. Somehow a good review in this case is not what I was after.

BETTY. This is all rather silly, isn't it?

ARCHIE. What is?

BETTY. The games. The finessing. The dress rehearsals. The unrealistic expectations. Jesus, we keep fooling ourselves.

ARCHIE. Think that's possible?

BETTY. What?

ARCHIE. To fool ourselves. That'd be like doing a card trick on ourselves. Not much point, right?

BETTY. Right.

ARCHIE. Back to the chess?

BETTY. How about cards?

ARCHIE. Good idea. I have the deck. What do you want to play?

BETTY. You pick it.

ARCHIE. Bridge?

BETTY. I don't know how.

ARCHIE. Neither do I, but I think we should give it a chance.

BETTY. Deal.

ARCHIE. How many cards?

BETTY. I like this. We are starting right from scratch, aren't we.

ARCHIE. Like first day of class.

BETTY. The tension, the anticipation, the wanting to do well, the slight cramping in the bowels, on the verge of praying, the ho…

ARCHIE. What?

BETTY. Nothing.

ARCHIE. *(pressing her)* No, what? What were you going to say?

BETTY. Nothing. Deal.

ARCHIE. You were going to say, "hoping," weren't you?

BETTY. Not at all.

ARCHIE. I think you're lying.

BETTY. *(embarrassed giggle)* You know me so well.

ARCHIE. How could I not.

BETTY. Okay, so I was going to say "hoping." But I didn't, did I? Not like some people I know and won't mention.

ARCHIE. Still, it's nice to know even you can almost fall into the trap.

BETTY. But I didn't.

ARCHIE. I'll let you have this one.

BETTY. You know what makes it difficult not to?

ARCHIE. Tell me.

BETTY. *(increasing a rant)* It seems it's all we have left. All these attempts at diversion don't work. We've spent hours at every board game, card game, word game known to man and it doesn't work. We've read every book in the library and even tried to write some of our own. We've had sex in every position known to Man or beast. Endless attempts, endless struggles to cope with the inevitable, but it doesn't work, does it?

ARCHIE. It certainly doesn't. *(beat)* What doesn't?

BETTY. The attempt to wipe out "hope."

ARCHIE. That's what I've been saying. It's all futile.

BETTY. What is?

ARCHIE. The attempts to wipe out hope.

BETTY. But if we don't, it's all so futile.

ARCHIE. What is?

BETTY. Hoping.

ARCHIE. So you're saying…

BETTY. Either way we're screwed. We can't live with it, we can't live without it.

ARCHIE. *(astounded)* You're right!

BETTY. So we are back at that point.

ARCHIE. We've reached my turn?

BETTY. Do it.

(**ARCHIE** *takes out a gun and shoots* **BETTY.** **BETTY** *falls over at the table.* **ARCHIE** *stares at* **BETTY** *for a protracted time. He looks around, then walks around, then returns to the chair. He sits and waits. He checks out* **BETTY.** *He continues to stare at her for a while, then slowly, and reluctantly, picks up the cards and begins to play solitaire.* **BETTY** *slowly awakens.* **ARCHIE,** *relieved, begins to deal the cards as the lights close to black.)*

The End

PUMPS

PUMPS is an adaptation of "William", a short story by the playwright, originally published in the *Santa Barbara Review*.

CAST

ACTOR

SETTING

Empty stage

(AT LIGHTS: **ACTOR** *enters.)*

ACTOR. I've made a careful, analytical study of pumps. I know about centrifugal, rotary, hydraulic, diesel, oil, baling, gasoline, and air pressured pumps. But the pump which holds the most interest for me is my own heart. Many's the hour I spend, stethoscope in hand, one end in my ears, the other on my chest, listening to the steady, inevitable, pulsation of my heart. I can differentiate the "lub" sound of the tricuspid and mitral valves snapping shut, and then the "dub" sound when the pulmonary and aortic valves jump into action. "Lub," "dub," "lub," "dub," "lub," "dub," endlessly, a perpetual motion machine. Well, maybe not perpetual. *(beat)* I am a prisoner to the sounds of my own heart. "Lub," "dub," my heart sings to me as my blood courses its way around my body, returning to its origin, my heart. Contract, empty, relax, fill. Contract, empty, relax, fill. Round and round goes my blood, endlessly being sent on its way. *(beat)* I think my absorption with my heart began the night my father left the house to take his daily two mile walk after dinner. *(beat)* He never returned. I was ten at the time. *(beat)* When my father was found several hours later with several holes in his body made by bullets from a small bore pistol shot by an unknown assailant for no known reason, my sheltered and comfortable life crumbled, my life's predictability and expectations shattered. *(beat)* The next day a rainstorm, vicious and tumultuous, began. As I watched the rainwater cascading from the roof of the building across from mine, huge puddles in the street formed from the melding and reforming of myriad smaller puddles. Rain lashed by powerful gusts of wind pelted the glass of my window, ricocheting

41

down onto the street below. Looking up, I could see immense black clouds streaking across the sky as they released their rain like warplanes on a strafing run. Night came and the street lights cast their yellowish tint to the deluge. I watched as the water fell in silvery sheets, glistening and shining in the light of the street lamps across from my window. The streets were empty as all hunkered down in their homes while the storm raged. *(beat)* Standing there I was in awe of the incomprehensible and irrational savagery of the raw nature beating around me. *(beat)* I sank into a revere thinking of all the storms I had seen, trying to comprehend the oceans of water that had fallen at exactly this very spot on the globe since the beginning of time. Before there was tar to build the roads, concrete to build the sidewalks, wood and steel to build the buildings, when the ground was earth and the earth could absorb the tons of water, would the rains have cleansed or simply turned the earth to mud? Was the earth on my father's grave turning to mud? Was the water seeping into his coffin? Was the box filling with water, overflowing, threatening to spill him out into the muddy grass? And what of all the others, the untold number of others spread throughout the cemeteries of the world, a diaspora of death? Were they being washed by the torrents of water pouring from the sky? At the day of reckoning would my father emerge cleansed of his wounds? *(beat)* It was at that moment I realized the key to regaining my equilibrium and harmony with the world, when I found that upon which I could always rely, that which would never fail me, which moved to an unchangeable rhythm no matter what equivalent of Scylla and Charybdis I may be passing through. No matter how much rain poured from the sky, no matter if it cleansed my father or not, I found what I needed to sustain my life. I found my heart.

(**ACTOR** *takes stethoscope from pocket, places it ears and over heart.*)

ACTOR. *(cont.)* And so now I sit listening to the "lub," "dub" of my heart, picturing the blood coursing mightily and healthily through my arteries and veins, and wondering sadly about the blood that poured from my father's wounds, wounds that caused my father's heart to stop.

The End

THE FINE PRINT

CAST

BILL
ELLEN
JOHN

PLACE

Bill and Ellen's living room

TIME

Now

SET

Interior of home. Living area. Door to offstage left. Door to outside right. Or maybe the other way around.

(AT LIGHTS: **BILL** *is seated in a chair reading a newspaper.)*

BILL. *(to offstage)* Says here scientists think in nine billion years the earth will be pulled into the sun and be destroyed. More problems.

ELLEN. *(from offstage)* What?

BILL. I think it's time to review our insurance policies.

*(***ELLEN*** enters holding a plant which she carefully, and admiringly, places on a table.)*

ELLEN. The water was running. I didn't hear you.

BILL. I said it might be time to review our insurance policies.

ELLEN. *(as she exits)* You do it. Those policies things drive me crazy.

*(***ELLEN*** exits.)*

BILL. Well, that wouldn't be too long a…

*(***ELLEN*** enters; ***BILL*** stops mid-sentence.)*

ELLEN. Don't even think about finishing that sentence.

BILL. Well, those policy things makes me nuts, too. *(***BILL*** puts up his hand, palm to ***ELLEN***, warning her not to respond)* But we should do it once in awhile. Particularly with the world coming to an end.

ELLEN. What are you talking about?

BILL. Never mind. Where are the policies?

ELLEN. I'll get them, but couldn't we do something a little more exciting, like watch the plant grow or take a nap.

BILL. Can you please get the policies?

*(***ELLEN*** exits. ***BILL*** returns to his reading. The doorbell rings. ***BILL*** goes to the door, at which stands ***JOHN***, well dressed, carrying a briefcase.)*

BILL. *(cont'd)* Yes?

JOHN. This *is* the Collin's house? William and Ellen Collins?

BILL. Yes.

JOHN. I've come about the payment.

BILL. What payment?

JOHN. May I come in? I have some papers here that pertain to you and your wife.

BILL. Are you selling anything, because if you are...

JOHN. No, no. This isn't an insurance scam and I'm not selling magazine subscriptions. May I?

BILL. *(hesitant, but finally...)* Yeah. For a minute. My wife and I were about...

JOHN. This really shouldn't take long. It's pretty routine, actually.

(**JOHN** *enters, looks around, sits. He opens his briefcase and takes out some papers which he places on the table.*)

This is all fairly straight forward. Your parents signed a document...let's see...*(looks at papers)*..fifty [*note: this can be altered to fit the age of actor playing* **BILL**] years ago...your birthday is March 20th, yesterday?

BILL. Right.

JOHN. Well, happy birthday.

BILL. Thanks. Now, what...

JOHN. So they signed this document fifty [*again, alter if necessary*] years ago on the day of your birth agreeing that on your fiftieth [*as above*] birthday you would begin to pay the standard fee of one half of one percent per month or six percent...

BILL. Per year. Yeah, I get it. What I don't get is what you mean by the standard fee and what you are doing here.

JOHN. The standard fee is the rent on everything you've accumulated throughout your life.

BILL. *(stunned)* Everything I've...*(stops)*

JOHN. *(laughing)* I get the same reaction every time. Yes, everything, Mr. Collins. *(emphatically)* Everything.

BILL. And this document was…

JOHN. *(handing* BILL *a piece of paper)* Your birth certificate.

(BILL *studies the paper. There is a long pause while they stare at each other. During the following,* BILL *is disbelieving,* JOHN *is bemused.)*

BILL. *(to offstage)* ELLEN.

ELLEN. *(from offstage)* I can't find them.

BILL. ELLLEN!

ELLEN. *(from offstage)* Stop screaming. I hear you. I said I can't find them.

BILL. ELLLLLEN!!

(ELLEN *enters.)*

ELLEN. What are you screaming…Who's this?

BILL. I don't know.

ELLEN. My husband doesn't know who you are, so perhaps you'll tell me.

(Lights dim for a couple of seconds, then relight. BILL *and* JOHN *are where they were,* ELLEN *is now seated in a chair.)*

ELLEN *(cont'd) (to* JOHN*)* You're out of your mind. Get out.

JOHN. Everyone says that to me, but if you'd look at the birth certificate *(hands it to* ELLEN*),* there at the very bottom…

(ELLEN *scrunches up her face, squints mightily and stares at the paper.)*

ELLEN. I'm supposed to read that?

(BILL *rushes off and returns quickly with a magnifying glass.)*

JOHN. There we go. Perfect. A magnifying glass.

(BILL *takes the paper and examines it under the magnifying glass.)*

BILL. I don't believe it.

(**ELLEN** *grabs the paper and the glass and reads. She slowly hands the paper back to* **JOHN**. **BILL** *and* **ELLEN** *are stunned.*)

JOHN. *(rubbing his hands in great glee)* I love this part.

BILL. It says something there about everything on load…

JOHN. On loan. Loan with an "n."

BILL. Ah, on loan, and that upon my death if I have no heirs…I got lost then, kind of. Never was too good with policy language.

JOHN. *(to* **BILL***)* What that means is, if you die first, whatever is jointly owned by the two of you stays with Ellen. Then when Ellen dies, if there are no heirs, whatever is here, all of it, comes to us. You have no children, correct?

BILL. Correct.

JOHN. Well, that's it then. It makes it much simpler. You die, she gets it; she dies, we get the whole shooting match. But until that day, you pay rent. Simple. *N'est-ce pas?*

BILL. *(suddenly in a rage)* N'EST-CE PAS? *(standing up)* I'll give you a *n'est-ce pas*. Get the fuck out of here.

JOHN. *(calmly)* Bill, Ellen, this won't do you any good. This is a binding contract. It's irrevocable, so calm down.

ELLEN. You just can't come in here with this cockamamie birth certificate scam and expect us to roll over. We own this stuff, this house, this car, this…this stuff.

JOHN. It's true you have all the legal papers that say so, the bills of sale, the mortgage, the receipts. But since the birth certificate predates all of that, all those papers mean is you can use this stuff for a while, but then it has to be turned over. To us. All of this is essentially a load… er…loan being leased with no buy out provision. Over is over. As the cliché says, you can't take it with you.

ELLEN. But we've lived in this house for nearly twenty years. The mortgage is paid up in ten. Then it's ours. The entire house and property. Ours; paid for fair and square.

JOHN. Were you the first owners?

ELLEN. No.

JOHN. So then someone was here before you.

ELLEN. The Cohens.

JOHN. That's right. We had a contract with them, too, of course. And eventually someone will live here after you. After you sell the house and move to where ever, someone else will be here. You agree?

BILL. Yeah, so?

JOHN. Well, then, you don't own the house. You own the right to stay in the house for however long you want or until you die, whichever comes first.

BILL. Ellen?

ELLEN. Calm down, Bill.

JOHN. We're not kicking you out. You have every legal right to stay here. Just so long as you understand you are staying here not as owners of the house, but as owners of the right to stay in the house. And we grant that right. Now: *N'est-ce pas?*

ELLEN. Not so fast, Slick.

JOHN. Slick? My name is John, not…

ELLEN. You keep talking about "we," "us." Just who are "we" and "us?"

(**JOHN** *waves his hand above his head as if to indicate the heavens.*)

ELLEN *(cont'd)* Really? God? You mean there really is…*(anxious)* Bill, those movies we took of us, you know, on our vacation last year…maybe we should…

JOHN. God? Movies? *(getting it, laughs)* Oh, you thought… Oh, no. No, I'm not from morals department. No, I'm from the real estate department. My department is on the asset side of the ledger. Those movies you and Bill took are on the debit side. Although if I saw them, I might change my mind on that *(laughs at his own joke).*

BILL. Then life is really just a matter of bookkeeping?

JOHN. From my perspective that's a decent analogy.

ELLEN. Wait a second. Bill didn't sign the certificate. His parents did. How can he be held responsible?

JOHN. Your wife has a keen legal mind, Bill. *(to* **ELLEN***)* In all other cases you're right, Ellen. In this case, the catch is if the DNA matches. *(proud of himself)* I just made up the little rhyme. Catches, matches. (**ELLEN** *and* **BILL** *don't respond)* Well, anyway, if it does…

BILL. Match?

JOHN. …then there's no way out. This contract is just like any other debt on an estate. It is in perpetuity. It goes on and on, until it doesn't. And that's when "we" step in to pick up the pieces.

ELLEN. *(to* **BILL***)* Your parents were schmucks.

JOHN. In fairness, the birth of a child is a confusing time. It's amazing how crazed people get.

ELLEN. And you take advantage of it, I'll bet.

JOHN. You'd win that bet, Ellen. I'll never forget the time…

ELLEN. Cram your war stories, John.

JOHN. I can understand you're upset, but there no reason to…

ELLEN. So what do we do now?

JOHN. Now? Now it's payment time. *(to* **BILL***)* Bill?

BILL. *(giving in)* How does this work?

(**JOHN** *presents a huge payment book.)*

JOHN. Do you remember the payment book you had for your car. Well….

(Lights out.)

The End

SILENCE

SILENCE premiered at Teachers Theatre's 2004 More Tears and Laughter One Act Play Festival. Subsequent performances were at New Jersey Dramatists 2004 Which Way to America One Act Play Festival; Jersey Voices, 2005 One Act Festival; Turtle Shell Production, 2007 8 Minute Madness Festival and Miami's City Theatre 2008 Summer Shorts Festival.

CAST

AARON - Eighteen years old
SARAH - Seen at 40 years of age, then at 60
ABEL - Seen at 40, then at 60

If casting permits, **SARAH** and **ABEL** should be thin and wan.

PLACE

Sarah's store, then Sarah and Abel's home

TIME

1948 and 1968

SETTING

Kitchen. Table, two chairs.

(*AT LIGHTS:* **AARON** *enters, stands to one side. He speaks only to the audience throughout the play.*)

AARON. After twenty years, Abel Gittle finally figured out a proper response to his life. It was April of 1968. Abel went to bed on a Wednesday night, said good night to his wife, Sarah, then woke up Thursday morning, committed to eternal silence.

(**SARAH** *[at age 60] enters and, with back to audience begins to prepare breakfast. After a few beats,* **ABEL** *[at age 60] enters and sits in a chair at the table.*)

AARON (*cont'd*) (*to coincide with* **ABEL**'s *entrance*) It was morning when Abel shuffled in and sat at the kitchen table.

SARAH. Abel, you want one egg or two?

(**ABEL** *lifts his right arm and with two fingers held aloft, signals his answer.*)

AARON. (*to coincide with above action*) Then he contentedly watched as Sarah busied herself preparing their breakfast, a task she had been doing since they were married, twenty years now, last October. By Abel's quick calculation, that made it 246 months.

ABEL. (*muttering to himself*) Weeks and days I'll figure out later.

SARAH. You want soft or hard?

(**ABEL** *waffles his arm in the air as if to indicate he didn't much care either way.*)

AARON. (*to coincide with above action*) Abel watched Sarah's thin legs sticking out below the hem of her house dress like translucent pipe cleaners.

ABEL. (*muttering to himself*) Thin legs. We all got such thin legs.

SARAH. Cat got your tongue, Mister? Meantime, 'stead of sitting, you could set the table.

(**ABEL** *stands and shuffles to the cabinet to get the two dishes, to the drawer to get the knives and forks, to the other cabinet to get the glasses for the tea.*)

ABEL. (*muttering to himself*) Makes it 1,066 weeks this Wednesday.

(**ABEL** *carefully lays out the dishes and utensils before sitting to watch* **SARAH** *make the breakfast.*)

SARAH. Those are not the dairy dishes.

AARON. If she sounds annoyed it may be the annoyance of a parent who has just explained to her child for the hundredth time why she keeps two sets of dishes.

(**ABEL** *smiles as he watches* **SARAH** *change the dishes.*)

SARAH. It may not be important for you, the dishes, but to me they're important. Now, toast?

(**ABEL** *nods in agreement.*)

Look, you gonna say something today, or can I take the hearing aids out from mine ears?

(**ABEL** *smiles and shrugs.*)

Abel, you are starting to make me crazy. Now, one piece toast or two and if you put up your fingers to tell me, you can make your own toast.

(**ABEL** *gets some bread from the package and puts them in the toaster. Then he sits again and smiles at a worried-looking* **SARAH**.)

Abel, you okay?

(**ABEL** *nods and smiles.*)

(**SARAH** *sits at the table. She wipes and re-wipes her hands on her apron, then she strokes his face and hair. She puts her hand to his brow to check for fever, then rolls down his eyelids to check for something. She looks intently into his face.*)

AARON. Abel had seen this look on Sarah's face only a few times before, this look of grief and fear, and he was sorry to see it now. He hadn't meant to cause her this pain, but he felt it was time for him to act. He...Wait.

To better understand this, perhaps we should go back twenty years.

(**ABEL** *exits.* **SARAH** *clears the table then stands behind the table, arms folded, waiting.*)

AARON *(cont'd)* When Abel got off the ship in 1947 he walked down the gangplank and into the first store he saw, a small dilapidated hole in the wall selling notions, thread and thimbles.

(**ABEL** *[at age 40], shabbily dressed, enters carrying a beat up suitcase tied with string.*)

AARON *(cont'd)* Inside he found Sarah and sensed he had found the right place.

(**SARAH** *[at age 40] stands resolutely but glumly behind the counter, her arms folded across her chest.* **SARAH** *peers intently into* **ABEL***'s face, then runs her eyes up and down his body. He stares a moment at her, then puts down his cord-bound cardboard suitcase. Without a word,* **SARAH** *exits into the back of the store.*)

(**SARAH** *exits.*)

AARON *(cont'd)* Abel sat and waited, hearing her bang around dishes and cups and whatnot. Finally, she emerged with a plate of sardines and tomatoes with a piece of black bread and a glass of tea which Abel nibbled and sipped during their initial chat.

(**SARAH** *enters carrying plates and glass of tea.*)

SARAH. From where?

ABEL. Lemberg. You?

SARAH. Warsaw.

ABEL. Nice. I visited a few times.

SARAH. More tea?

ABEL. Thank you.

(**SARAH** *exits.* **ABEL** *slowly indulges in the food.* **SARAH***, now with a shawl around her shoulders, enters having re-arranged her hair in a bun, applied rouge and lip-stick, all of which is met approvingly by* **ABEL***.*)

SARAH. So, you liked Warsaw?

ABEL. Too big.

(*They pause.*)

AARON. At this point Sarah waited. She knew these things took time. She had been in New York two years now. In Warsaw she had twenty girls working under her in the shoe factory, so a shop this size she could manage. Eating, sleeping, being with people, these would come later.

SARAH. You have a place?

ABEL. I'll find.

(**SARAH** *finds a piece of paper and pencil, writes, then hands the paper to* **ABEL.**)

SARAH. Call him. A man also from Lemberg. Here maybe a year.

(**ABEL** *keeps eating and sipping, each bite and sip savored, as he reads the paper.*)

ABEL. You sure Lemberg?

SARAH. Absolutely. No question. (*pause*) In Lemberg, you had work?

ABEL. I was an actor.

SARAH. Couldn't be you were an actor.

(**SARAH** *pulls up a chair and sits opposite* **ABEL.**)

ABEL. Could be and was. Why couldn't I be an actor?

SARAH. Actors talk. They speak words. You been in mine shop now an hour you ain't said more than six syllables.

(**ABEL** *stands and walks away from the table. He clears his throat. He speaks with an obviously theatrically trained voice.*)

ABEL. My life is over and done with. I'm gifted, intelligent, courageous. If I'd lived a normal life, I might have turned out as a Schopenhauer, a Dostoevsky. I'm talking so much nonsense. I'm going out of my mind. Matushka, I've lost heart and soul.

(ABEL stops, clears his throat and sits.)

SARAH. Those are the words you want to tell me?

ABEL. Those are my words.

(SARAH quickly collects the plates, the cutlery, the glass and napkin and takes them all into the back of the store. ABEL waits. SARAH enters.)

SARAH. Those weren't your words.

ABEL. How do you know?

SARAH. Look, Mister. You come into mine store and I right away give you food, sardines, bread, a glass of tea. And now you insult me.

ABEL. How insult you?

SARAH. I told you I am from Warsaw. I am not one of those *shtetel* peasants. I am a sophisticated lady. And I saw Uncle Vanya on the stage more than you gave performances of him. I know mine Chekhov. So don't give me with the "how do you know." I know plenty, Mister.

ABEL. I'll bet you do, and I apologize for any hard feelings I have caused.

SARAH. *(considers)* I accept.

(pause)

ABEL. So, know why I came into this shop?

SARAH. No.

ABEL. Me neither. But must have been a reason. Luck like this I never had before.

SARAH. You mean with women.

ABEL. I mean with life. So, more tea?

AARON. Abel and Sarah were married nearly twenty years when, at the age of eighteen, and six months after the diagnosis of lymphoma, I was dead and Abel and Sarah had to buy me a burial plot and a coffin. Late into the night, as they sat in their small apartment, unable to face not thinking about their son, unwilling to let my image go even for sleep, Abel and Sarah tried to work it out.

ABEL. *(at age 60)* You'll excuse me, but Aaron dying reminds me of the camp.

SARAH. *(at age 60)* You're crazy.

ABEL. I'm crazy? Maybe. No. I agree, I'm crazy. But want to know how? Want to know why Aaron dying is like the camp?

SARAH. Okay, scholar. Why our son dying like the camp?

(During the following speech, **ABEL** *leaps from the chair and begins to pace, then building to a frenzy, rushes around the stage.)*

ABEL. Because it don't make no sense. It was like that, right? You remember. No sense. Me, him, them, today, tomorrow, the day after, eat, don't eat, drink, don't drink, shit, don't shit, don't never make no difference because it never made any sense. Words, words, words, no words could ever make it make sense. No sense, no rhyme, no reason.

*(*ABEL *continues to pace and mutely gesture during the following narration.)*

AARON. Sarah silently watched as Abel ranted. For twenty years they had a pact: there would be no talk of the camps, only silence. Whenever the subject surfaced, in movies, in books, on TV, in the news, Abel and Sarah lived up to the rules of their unspoken agreement and made no acknowledgment that any of that had ever meant anything to them. They could have been listening to stories about Mars or Jupiter for all the reaction they would have. Until now.

ABEL. Never made sense, never fair. All the time there, never saw anything I could understand. It was like walking around in a room pitch black run by crazy men without hearts or brains. Now this, this…. We talk to doctors about Aaron and they talk to doctors who talk to doctors, and they all reassure us and six months later he is dead. I'll tell you, Sarah, this place is scarier than that place. Know why? I said…

SARAH. *(resigned)* No, Abel, I don't know why. Tell me.

(**ABEL** *leans over her, his face not more than inches from her.* **SARAH** *keeps her eyes closed, waiting.*)

ABEL. There they said nothing and they killed. Here they talk, they talk and talk and they lie and they don't know nothing and you die anyway. There there was no hope so you knew what was going to happen. Here there is first hope and then your brains are beaten out. There we counted the days we stayed alive. Here we count the days until we die and then we figure the days, the weeks, the months, the years since someone died and we light a candle. There was better. Each day when we counted we knew we had lasted one more day.

(After a pause to let this sink in, **SARAH** *slowly stands and begins to exit.)*

AARON. *(to coincide with above action)* It was two in the morning. It was two weeks past the *shiva,* but since time didn't measure her feelings, that didn't mean much to Sarah.

ABEL. Where you going?

SARAH. What you care?

ABEL. *(surprised)* What I care? I care. I care plenty.

SARAH. Fah! You care. Fah!

ABEL. How can you say I don't care?

SARAH. You care, you don't speak to me that way. You don't tell me what happened to Aaron is worse than the camps. You don't speak to me like that.

ABEL. You saying I'm wrong?

SARAH. No, you sad, old man. I don't disagree. You are right. You are dead right. This is worse. That's why you have some nerve ever speaking to me like that.

AARON. It was that night my father decided he had spoken enough. It was right after he figured it was 7,462 days.

The End

POP GOES THE WEASEL

POP GOES THE WEASEL premiered at Harbor Theatre's 2001 One-Act Play Festival, Harbor Currents, directed by Amanda Selwyn.

CAST

ACTOR 1
ACTOR 2
ACTOR 3
CD

TIME

Now

PLACE

Anywhere

SETTING

Three chairs lined up facing the audience. There is a table to one side on which sits a cd-player.

(AT LIGHTS: Three ACTORS sit on the three chairs. A fourth actor, CD, stands at the CD-player. CD starts the cd-player and we hear: POP GOES THE WEASEL. The three ACTORS stand and begin to circle the chairs.)

ACTOR 1. Well, hello.

ACTOR 2. Well, hello to you. *(to ACTOR 3)* And to you.

ACTOR 3. Nice to see you.

ACTOR 1. How have you been?

ACTOR 2. Just fine. And you?

ACTOR 3. Couldn't be better.

ACTOR 2. You're both looking well.

ACTOR 1. And you never get a day older.

ACTOR 2. I wish that were true.

(CD slowly drags one of the chairs off-stage.)

ACTOR 3. Aging happens so quickly.

ACTOR 2. Before you know it.

ACTOR 1. Aging is better than the alternative.

ACTOR 2. Anything is better than the alternative.

(All of the ACTORS become aware of the moving chair. As they speak and move around the stage, they become increasingly agitated.)

ACTOR 3. The alternative is so final.

ACTOR 1. The alternative is so frightening.

ACTOR 3. Well, I must be going.

ACTOR 1. Oh, I hope not.

ACTOR 2. Nice to know you're still around.

(All the ACTORS begin to move toward the two remaining chairs.)

ACTOR 3. Best to...

ACTOR 2. Right...

ACTOR 1. Gotta go.

ACTOR 3. Me, too.

(CD stops the music. All three ACTORS rush to the two remaining chairs, but only two sit. ACTOR 1 is left standing. Stage goes to black, then quickly lights. ACTOR 1 is gone. The two remaining ACTORS sit in their chairs and give furtive glances to CD and to each other. The music starts and the ACTORS begin to circle the chairs.)

ACTOR 2. Did you see that?

ACTOR 3. Very scary.

ACTOR 2. Awful.

(ACTOR 3 places an offering in front of CD then walks on.)

ACTOR 2 *(cont'd) (indicates the offering)* Think that will do any good?

ACTOR 3. Hard to know.

ACTOR 2. Think I should?

ACTOR 3. I'm not sure.

ACTOR 2. Maybe I'll wait to see what happens.

ACTOR 3. By then it might be too late.

ACTOR 2. Might be too little.

ACTOR 3. Hard to know.

ACTOR 2. Hard to think.

(CD begins to drag another chair off-stage. The ACTORS, responding more quickly this time, begin to edge toward the chairs.)

ACTOR 3. Shame about...you know.

ACTOR 2. I guess that's how these things happen.

ACTOR 3. You mean when the music stops...

ACTOR 2. Right. That's when...

(The music stops. ACTORS rush for the remaining chair. ACTOR 2 sits. ACTOR 3 is left to stand, looking around frantically and begins to cry. ACTOR 2 at first looks sympathetic, then averts face while fiercely holding on to the chair. The stage goes to black, then quickly re-lights. ACTOR 3 is gone. ACTOR 2 intensely watches CD who stands by the CD-player. CD starts the music.)

ACTOR 2 *(cont'd) (to the audience)* If that *(points to* **CD***)* is a harbinger, it appears a major change is in the forecast. There's a lot of blather about the various stages of Man, but, in fact, there is only one stage. And this is it *(points down)*, the one and only, the start and finish, the alpha, the omega, the....

(**ACTOR 2**, *holding chair, walks to* **CD** *and carefully looks* **CD** *over.* **CD** *ignores* **ACTOR 2** *who takes a deck of cards from pocket.*)

ACTOR 2 *(cont'd)* Pick a card.

(No reaction from **CD**.*)*

Don't be shy. It's called the disappearing card trick. Kind of like what you do except with cards instead of people. Go on, pick one.

(**CD** *does not react.* **ACTOR 2** *gives it up and returns down-stage.*)

Doesn't look good. *(beat)* I'd write a will, but I have nothing of value to leave. I'm taking whatever is of value with me, and it's all up here *(points to head)*. When I go, it goes. I am defined by this brain, and what this brain knows. Dead, it knows nothing. If I am my brain and my brain knows nothing, then before you stands a potential zero. *(beat)* How mortifying!

(**ACTOR 2**, *holding chair, returns to* **CD** *and tries to entertain* **CD** *with a dance [actor's choice] which* **CD** *ignores.* **ACTOR 2** *quits and returns downstage.*)

Tough audience. *(beat)* Ah, what a waste. I ask you, what was the point of all these years, all this...this...living if in the end it comes down to this...this clinging to one measly little chair? ENRAGING ISN'T IT. *(pause)* Sorry. It's just that I have a lot on my mind. Primarily that *(indicates* **CD***), with that music thing. (pause)* Who the fuck *is* that and where does it get off...?

(**ACTOR 2**, *carrying chair, begins to move threateningly toward* **CD** *who begins to move toward the CD-player.* **ACTOR 2** *freezes.* **CD** *stops.* **ACTOR 2** *sits.*)

ACTOR 2 *(cont'd)* Close one. *(beat)* Haven't been sleeping well lately. Appetite a bit off, too. Sex isn't what it used to be, either. But there was a time...I used to love that feeling right at the end of sex, right when things go blotto, where the rest of the world is blocked out, like just before you go to sleep, it's just me and my head and my thoughts and then there's no thoughts, just feeling, and then...oblivion.

*(***ACTOR 2*** stands, takes the chair, and walks to* **CD**.*)*

(to **CD***)* OBLIVION! Do you have anything to say on that matter? *(to audience)* This is starting to piss me off. *(beat)* I think the difference is with sex and sleep I trust I'll be back. With this damn thing... Ah, what's the use? From what I've seen around here there's no point to struggle. Might as well roll over, hope for the best. Do not go gentle into that good night? Well, why the hell not? Rage, rage against the dying of the light. Hah! Think about it. All those screams of rage of all those people in all those years. Like a fart in a wind-storm. I never was a passive kind of person, but in this case... I know hopeless when I see it. *(beat)* Still, given what's at stake, I guess it's worth one more try. *(to* **CD***)* Look, any chance of buying a little more time? Doesn't have to be much. I'm negotiable.

*(***CD*** begins tugging the chair to the wings.* **ACTOR 2** *struggles to keep a hold on the chair. The struggle goes on throughout the following.)*

You know, time! Years, months, weeks, days, hours, minutes, seconds. TIME!

(More struggling.)

Clocks, calendars. TIME!

(Eventually, despite attempt to keep the chair on stage, **ACTOR 2** *is pulled off stage by* **CD**. **CD** *returns, stands by CD-player, stares at audience as lights slowly fade to blackout.)*

The End

PROPERTY AND COSTUME LIST

DOG YEARS

Property:
Clip board
Paper
Pencil

Costume:
Psychotherapist: Jacket/shirt/tie

COMRADES

Property:
Hospital bed
Bandages
Blanket

Costume:
Whatever clothed a Russian
 peasant in the 1850s.

THE SUITCASE

Property:
Clipboard
Paper

Costume:
Whatever is appropriate for
 arranging a funeral.

LUCKY MAN

Property:
Doctor's charts
Medium size slab of red meat

Costume:
White doctor's coat

REHEARSAL

Property:
Chess set
Gun
Deck of cards

PUMPS

Property:
Stethoscope

THE FINE PRINT

Property:
Potted plant
Briefcase
Papers
Magnifying glass
Huge payment book

SILENCE

Property:
4 plates/knives and forks
Napkins
Packaged bread
Toaster
Apron
Beat up suitcase tied with string
Sliced tomato
Black bread
Glass for tea
Paper
Pencil

Costume:
Man and Woman's bathrobes
Bedroom slippers for each
Kitchen apron
Shabby man's jacket
Woman's shawl

POP GOES THE WEASEL

Property:
CD player
Object used for offering to the
Gods
Deck of cards

Also by
Henry Meyerson...

Beware the Man Eating Chicken

Fresh Brewed:
Tales from the Coffee Bar

Shtick

Please visit our website **samuelfrench.com** for complete
descriptions and licensing information

Printed in the United States
212140BV00004B/4/P

9 780573 696213